Tigers in Terai

Tigers in Terai

BY

Amanda Lumry

AND

Laura Hurwitz

ILLUSTRATED BY

Sarah McIntyre

SCHOLASTIC PRESS ★ NEW YORK

Tibet
BHUTAN
Mt. Everest
Nepal
Kathmandu
Bardia
Chitwan
Kosi Tappu
TERAI
BANGLADESH
India
Calcutta
Bay of Bengal

Dear Riley,

Greetings, Carrot Top! Your Aunt Martha, Cousin Alice, and I are so excited you could join us in Nepal. We have some detective work to do!

Like tigers everywhere, the Bengal tigers in the Terai region of Nepal and India are **endangered**. They are running out of space to live and need more room to roam. We must find them and study their habits so we can figure out ways to help them survive.

Be sure to bring your camera and **binoculars**, since tigers are tricky to spot! I'll see you in **Kathmandu**!

Your favorite scientist,

Uncle Max

"Wow!" said Riley. "The mountains are taller than the clouds!"

"Welcome to **Kathmandu**!" said Uncle Max. "We're in the Himalayas, the highest mountain range in the world. Just one more flight and we'll be in Terai, the lowlands of Nepal."

After landing in Terai, Riley and Alice walked over to see the local crafts. A carved tiger caught Riley's eye. He really wanted it, but he didn't have enough money.

"Riley! Alice!" called Uncle Max. "I'm glad you've already spotted a tiger, but we need to keep moving! Everyone at the **lodge** is waiting for us."

The road ended at a sparkling river.

"These boats will take us across," said Uncle Max.

"Hop in!" said Aunt Martha. "But watch out for crocodiles!"

When they reached the **lodge**, a young woman named Penny showed them around.

"We haven't seen too many tigers lately, and we're getting really worried," she said.

"I hope I see a tiger!" said Riley, running ahead.

"It's time for an elephant ride!" said Uncle Max, unpacking his camera traps and other supplies. "I need to place these special cameras around the jungle. They take pictures whenever something crosses in front of them."

"Cool!" said Riley and Alice.

At the loading platform, Riley and Alice carefully climbed onto the very large elephant.

"My name is Mohan," said the man on the elephant. "And my elephant's name is Kanchi."

Asian Elephant

- Twice the distance around an Asian elephant's footprint is equal to its height.
- It uses its trunk and feet to "hear" sounds through the ground made by other elephants.
- It feeds for 16 hours a day.

—Eric Wikramanayake,
Senior Conservation Scientist,
World Wildlife Fund

"This is more fun than riding in a car," said Riley.

"Elephants are wonderful, but they require constant attention," said Mohan. "I have to feed Kanchi even in the middle of night."

Suddenly, they heard someone yelling for help.

"Oh no!" said Riley. "I think someone is being chased by a tiger!"

"It's okay," said Uncle Max. "That's just a peafowl call."

Riley quickly took a picture, while Alice laughed and wrote about Riley's little scare in her journal.

Rhinoceros

- It has poor eyesight, so it uses its sense of smell to get around.
- Its horn is made of a special kind of tough hair, not bone!
- It holds the world's record for the single largest poop!

—Eric Dinerstein, Chief Scientist, Vice President for Science, World Wildlife Fund

"There's a rhinoceros up ahead!" said Riley.

"There may be tigers around, too," said Uncle Max. "Look at the fresh scratches on the tree. I'll put a camera trap here when the rhinoceros leaves."

After dinner, they went back to their rooms.

"What a mess!" exclaimed Uncle Max.

"What happened?" asked Alice.

"I don't know," said Uncle Max, "but my **sample containers** are missing. Without them, I can't collect hair or **dung** samples. That's how I identify individual tigers and what they eat."

In the morning, everyone went looking for the missing **sample containers** and to check on the camera traps. Mishra, Mohan's younger brother, joined the search.

"Look at those big black birds," said Alice.

"Those are called Indian flying foxes," said Uncle Max. "But they're actually bats."

"Oh," said Alice.

"I wonder if the camera trap took pictures of them?" asked Riley. He ran to catch up with Mishra.

Indian Flying Fox

- An Indian flying fox has a wingspan of 4 ft. (1.2 m) and is the world's largest bat.
- It is good at remembering the location of fruit trees and when the fruit is ripe.
- It does not eat the fruit itself, only the juice.

—Don E. Wilson,
Senior Scientist,
Smithsonian Institution

They crept quietly through the reeds to watch some grazing chital deer.

"Looking for animals is fun," said Mishra. "But I hope we don't see any tigers."

Chital Deer

- A chital deer is a good swimmer.
- It stays near monkeys, waiting to eat the fruit they drop.
- It can run up to 40 mph (64 km/h)—especially when it is being chased by a tiger!

—George Amato, Director,
Science Resource Center,
Wildlife Conservation Society

"Why not?" asked Riley.

"Tigers killed some of my family's goats," said Mishra.

"That's so sad!" said Riley. "My uncle is studying tigers so he can make more room for them to roam, far away from goats and people."

All of a sudden, something blue ran in front of them and up a nearby tree.

"Hey, Dad," called Alice. "That monkey is wearing your underwear!"

"That must be the little rascal who sneaked into my room and went through my suitcase!" said Uncle Max.

As the monkey ran off, Riley noticed Uncle Max's **sample containers**. He scampered up the tree and rescued them. "Now we can complete our mission!" said Uncle Max.

Hanuman Langur Monkey

- It enjoys spending time together in large groups.
- It can leap 33 ft. (10 m) high and 16 ft. (5 m) across.
- It has only one baby at a time.

—Dr. Cathi Lehn, Conservation Biologist, Science Resource Center, Wildlife Conservation Society

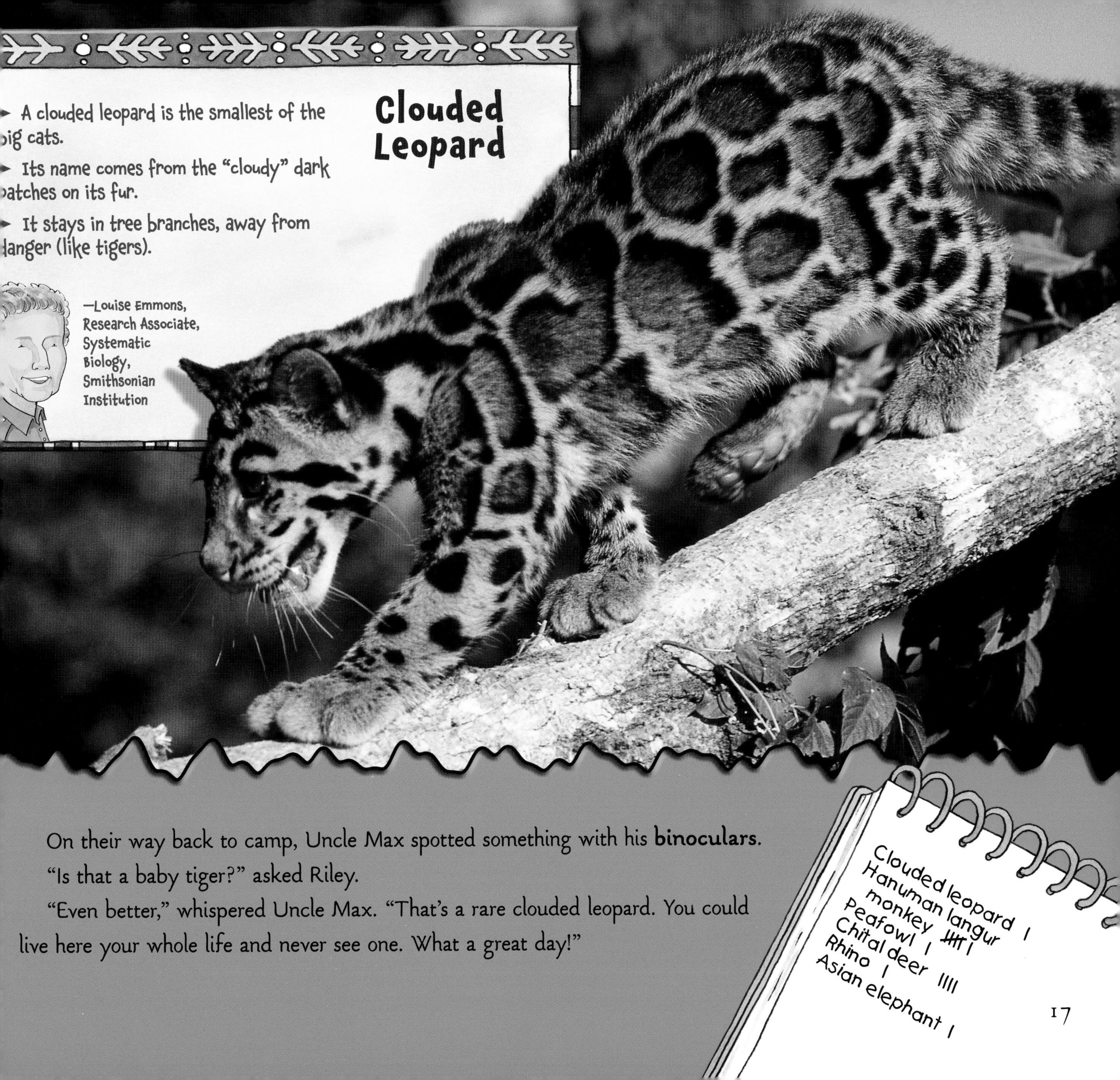

Clouded Leopard

- A clouded leopard is the smallest of the big cats.
- Its name comes from the "cloudy" dark patches on its fur.
- It stays in tree branches, away from danger (like tigers).

—Louise Emmons,
Research Associate,
Systematic
Biology,
Smithsonian
Institution

On their way back to camp, Uncle Max spotted something with his **binoculars**.

"Is that a baby tiger?" asked Riley.

"Even better," whispered Uncle Max. "That's a rare clouded leopard. You could live here your whole life and never see one. What a great day!"

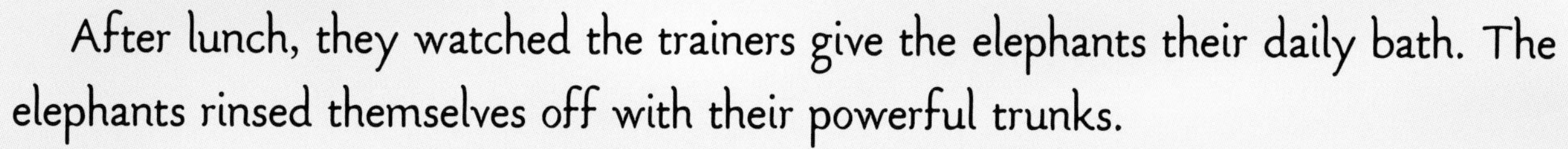

After lunch, they watched the trainers give the elephants their daily bath. The elephants rinsed themselves off with their powerful trunks.

"What a sight!" said Uncle Max, leaning closer.
SPLASH! A baby elephant sprayed water all over him.
"I guess you won't need a shower today!" said Alice.

While Riley was waiting for everyone to dry off, he noticed a small pouch under a bush. He bent down to pick it up. It was full of coins. Now he had enough money to buy that carved tiger!

He heard a soft rustling sound behind him. Peeking through the leaves, he saw something black and orange disappear into the jungle. He ran off to find the others.

Tiger

➤ Don't look for a tiger in Africa! Tigers only live in the hot, tropical forests of southern Asia and the cold, arctic plains of Siberia.

➤ A tiger is the largest member of the big cats (including lions).

—Dr. Anup Joshi,
Ecologist,
World Wildlife Fund

That night, Riley
dreamed of
tigers.

In the morning, they went on another jungle walk to collect **dung** and hair samples and check camera traps.

KAK-KAK! KAK-KAK!

"What's that?" asked Riley.

"That's a Great Indian Hornbill," Penny said, "and it's announcing its **presence**. Or maybe there is danger nearby."

"Um . . . is that danger over there?" whispered Alice.
Uncle Max shouted, "KING COBRA!" and then ushed everyone out of the way.

Sloth Bear

➤ A sloth bear sucks insects into its mouth through a space between its teeth. (That's worse than slurping your soup!)

➤ These eating noises can be heard from 330 ft. (100 m) away.

➤ It has pale fur on its chest in the shape of a "U," "V," or "Y."

—Robert S. Hoffmann,
Senior Scientist,
Smithsonian Institution

"Let's take the jeep to the next camera trap," suggested Uncle Max. After everyone climbed aboard, he drove them down a long and dusty dirt road.

"At least now the snakes can't get us," said Alice.

"But the bears still can!" said Uncle Max. A giant sloth bear appeared next to the road as the passed by. "That was close!"

"Uncle Max, there's some fresh tiger **dung** over here," Riley said.

"Great!" said Uncle Max, stopping the jeep. "I bet there's a lot of good tiger shots on this roll of film. Hooray!"

"Ah . . . Dad!" gulped Alice. "T-t-tiger!"

At the sound of Alice's voice, the big cat looked over. Uncle Max leaped into the front seat . . . JUST IN TIME! They held their breath as the tiger slowly crept across the road and then seemed to melt back into the tall grass.

"Wasn't that fantastic?" said Uncle Max. "I'm still shaking."

"So are we," said Riley and Alice.

"We can't let this **species** become **extinct**," said Aunt Martha. "We need to find a way for both people and tigers to share this land."

At the **lodge**, Riley and Alice ran to find Mohan and Mishra.

"We finally saw a tiger!" Riley said. Mishra tried to smile.

"What's wrong?" asked Alice.

"I lost my money pouch. My parents count on me to help out," said Mishra.

"Oh, is this your pouch?" asked Riley, reaching into his pocket. "I found it by the river."

"Yes, thank you!" said Mishra.

Just before they left to catch their plane, Mishra surprised them with gifts he had made: a carved tiger for Riley and a beaded necklace for Alice. They thanked Mishra and said good-bye to all of their new friends.

АКВАРИУМ
BING BOING
MONO-PULLY
KATHMANDU
LOONY PLANET

Back at home, Riley entertained his family with stories of the tiger, Mishra, and the monkey that stole Uncle Max's underwear. He made a place for the special wooden tiger and returned to living the life of a nine-year-old . . . until his mom handed him a new letter from Uncle Max.

Where will Riley go next?

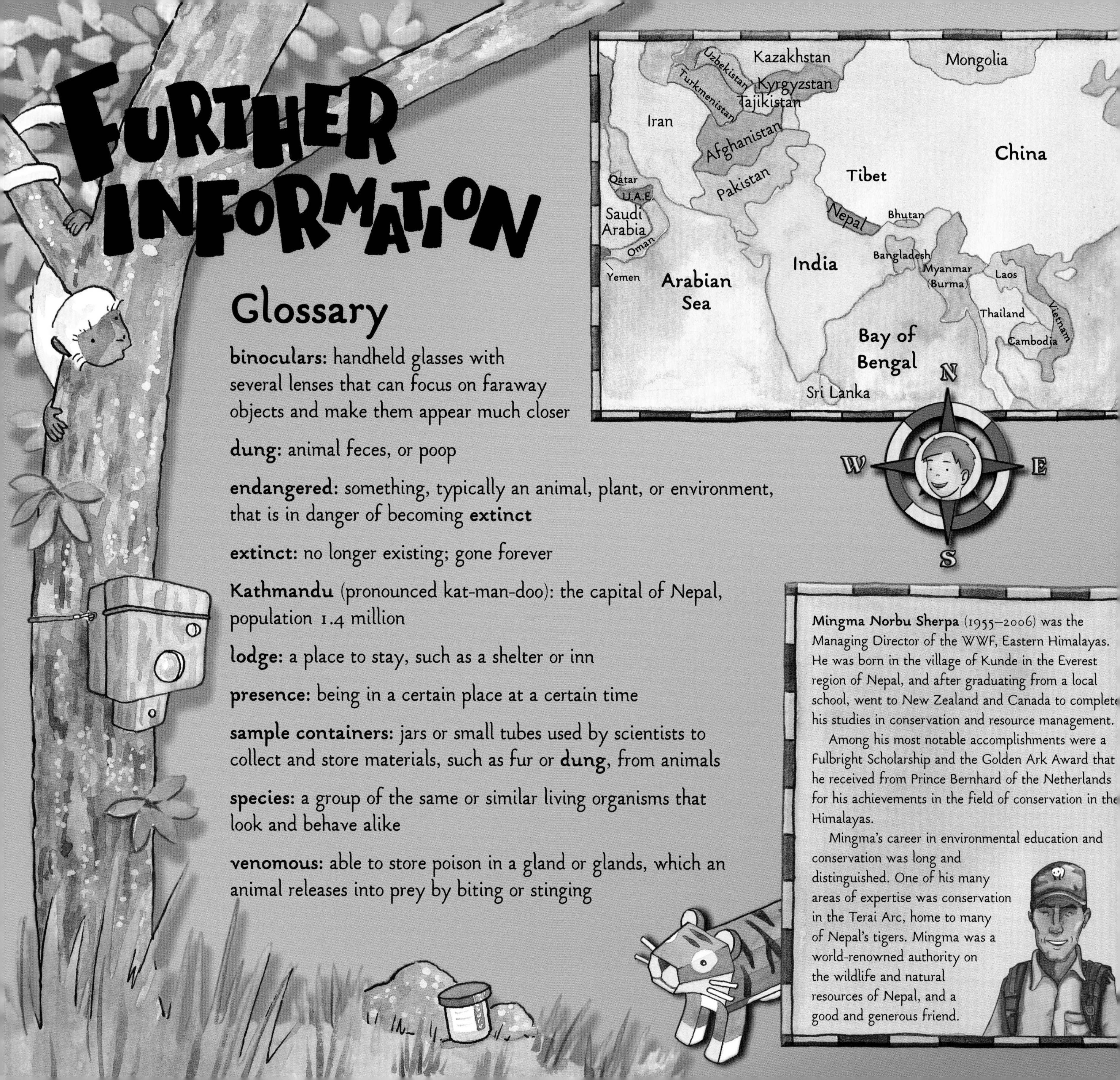

Further Information

Glossary

binoculars: handheld glasses with several lenses that can focus on faraway objects and make them appear much closer

dung: animal feces, or poop

endangered: something, typically an animal, plant, or environment, that is in danger of becoming **extinct**

extinct: no longer existing; gone forever

Kathmandu (pronounced kat-man-doo): the capital of Nepal, population 1.4 million

lodge: a place to stay, such as a shelter or inn

presence: being in a certain place at a certain time

sample containers: jars or small tubes used by scientists to collect and store materials, such as fur or **dung**, from animals

species: a group of the same or similar living organisms that look and behave alike

venomous: able to store poison in a gland or glands, which an animal releases into prey by biting or stinging

Mingma Norbu Sherpa (1955–2006) was the Managing Director of the WWF, Eastern Himalayas. He was born in the village of Kunde in the Everest region of Nepal, and after graduating from a local school, went to New Zealand and Canada to complete his studies in conservation and resource management.

Among his most notable accomplishments were a Fulbright Scholarship and the Golden Ark Award that he received from Prince Bernhard of the Netherlands for his achievements in the field of conservation in the Himalayas.

Mingma's career in environmental education and conservation was long and distinguished. One of his many areas of expertise was conservation in the Terai Arc, home to many of Nepal's tigers. Mingma was a world-renowned authority on the wildlife and natural resources of Nepal, and a good and generous friend.

JOIN US FOR MORE GREAT ADVENTURES!

RILEY'S WORLD

Visit our Web site at
www.adventuresofriley.com
to find out how
you can join Riley's
super kids' club!

Look for these other great Riley books:

- Safari in South Africa
- Project Panda
- South Pole Penguins
- Polar Bear Puzzle
- Dolphins in Danger

A special thank-you to all the scientists who collaborated on this project. Your time and assistance are very much appreciated.

First published in China in 2003 by Eaglemont Press.
www.eaglemont.com

All photographs by Amanda Lumry except:
Cover Bengal tiger, page 20 Bengal tiger, pages 26–27 Bengal tiger, and page 30 Bengal tiger © Joseph Van Os/Getty Images
Page 3 Dahaban, Nepal © Jonathan Alpeyrie/Getty Images
Page 9 peafowl © Michael Melford/Getty Images
Page 10 rhinoceros and page 24 sloth bear © Anup Shah/Getty Images
Page 17 clouded leopard © Tom Brakefield/Getty Images

Illustrations © 2003 by Sarah McIntyre
Additional Illustrations and Layouts by Ulkutay and Ulkutay, London WC2E 9RZ
Editing and Digital Compositing by Michael E. Penman
Digital Imaging by Embassy Graphics, Canada and Phoenix Color

Library of Congress Control Number: 2006031927

ISBN-13: 978-0-545-06842-0
ISBN-10: 0-545-06842-8

10 9 8 7 6 5 4 3 2 1   09 10 11 12 13

Printed in Singapore   46
First Scholastic printing, April 2009

A portion of the proceeds from your purchase of this licensed product supports the stated educational mission of the Smithsonian Institution—"the increase and diffusion of knowledge." The name of the Smithsonian Institution and the sunburst logo are registered trademarks of the Smithsonian Institution and are registered in the U.S. Patent and Trademark Office. www.si.edu

2% of the proceeds from this book will be donated to the Wildlife Conservation Society. http://wcs.org

An average royalty of approximately 3 cents from the sale of each book in the Adventures of Riley series will be received by World Wildlife Fund (WWF) to support their international efforts to protect endangered species and their habitats. ® WWF Registered Trademark Panda Symbol © 1986 WWF. © 1986 Panda symbol WWF-World Wide Fund For Nature (also known as World Wildlife Fund) ® "WWF" is a WWF Registered Trademark © 1986 WWF-Fonds Mondial pour la Nature symbole du panda Marque Déposée du WWF ®
www.worldwildlife.org

We try to produce the most beautiful books possible and we are extremely concerned about the impact of our manufacturing process on the forests of the world and the environment as a whole. Accordingly, we made sure that the paper used in this book has been certified as coming from forests that are managed to ensure the protection of the people and wildlife dependent upon them.

September 23, 2006 | **In memory of those who dedicated their lives to conservation in Nepal**

Dr. Bijnan Acharya
Program Development Specialist of USAID, Nepal

Margaret Alexander
Deputy Director of the USAID, Nepal

Hem Raj Bhandari
Reporter- Nepal Television

Dr. Chandra Prasad Gurung
Country Representative, WWF Nepal

Dr. Harka Gurung
Advisor, WWF Nepal

Jennifer Headley
Coordinator, Himalaya/South Asia Program, WWF UK

Yeshi Choden Lama
Senior Program Officer, WWF Nepal

Dr. Tirtha Man Maskey
Former Director General of Department of National Parks and Wildlife Conservation

Pauli Mustonen
Chargé d'Affaires, Embassy of Finland, Nepal

Dr. Damodar Parajuli
Acting Secretary, Ministry of Forests and Soil Conservation

Matthew Preece
Program Officer, Eastern Himalayas Program, WWF US

Narayan Poudel
Director General, Department of National Parks and Wildlife Conservation

Honorable Mr. Gopal and Mrs. Meena Rai
Minister of State, Ministry of Forests and Soil Conservation and his wife

Sharad Rai
Director General, Department of Forests

Dr. Jillian Bowling Schlaepfer
Director of Conservation, WWF UK

Mingma Norbu Sherpa
Managing Director, Eastern Himalayas Program, WWF US

Vijaya Shrestha
Central Committee Member, Federation of Nepalese Chamber of Commerce and Industry

Sunil Singh
Cameraman, Nepal Television

Dawa Tshering
Chairperson, Kangchenjunga Conservation Area Management Council

Klim Kim
Mingma Sherpa
Tandu Shrestha
Valery Slafronov
Flight Crew

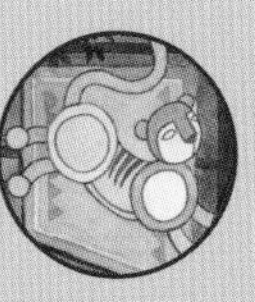